RIDE A COCK-HORSE
TO BANBURY CROSS

NEW ORCHARD EDITIONS

POOLE   DORSET

RIDE a Cock-Horse

to Banbury Cross,

To see a fine Lady

Get on a white Horse,

With rings on her fingers,

and bells on her toes,

She shall have music wherever she goes.

A FARMER WENT TROTTING

UPON HIS GREY MARE

A FARMER went trotting upon his grey Mare;
Bumpety, bumpety, bump!
With his Daughter behind him, so rosy and fair;
Lumpety, lumpety, lump!

A Raven cried "Croak!" and they all tumbled down;

Bumpety, bumpety, bump!

The Mare broke her knees, and the Farmer his crown;

Lumpety, lumpety, lump!

The mischievous Raven flew laughing away;
Bumpety, bumpety, bump!
And vowed he would surprise them the very next day;
Lumpety, lumpety, lump!

ISBN 1-85079-125-2

Printed in Portugal by Printer Portugesa